Fred's Ted

by Clare De Marco

Illustrated by Melanie Sharp

Notes on the series

TIDDLERS are structured to provide support for newly independent readers. The stories may also be used by adults for sharing with young children.

Starting to read alone can be daunting. **TIDDLERS** help by listing the words in the book for a check before reading, and by providing visual support and repeating words and phrases. These books will both develop confidence and encourage reading and rereading for pleasure.

If you are reading this book with a child, here are a few suggestions:

1. Make reading fun! Choose a time to read when you and the child are relaxed and have time to share the story.
2. Talk about the story before you start reading. Look at the cover and the blurb. What might the story be about? Why might the child like it?
3. Look also at the list of words below - can the child tackle most of the words?
4. Encourage the child to retell the story, using the jumbled picture puzzle.
5. Give praise! Remember that small mistakes need not always be corrected.

Here is a list of the words in this story.

Common words:

a	him	oh	too
big	I	put	will
but	into	said	
can	little	she	
got	Mum	some	
had	no	then	

Other words:

bed	fixed	rip	thread
call	Fred	stuffing	used
fix	much	Ted	

Little Ted had a rip.

"Oh no!" said Fred.

"I can fix him,"
said Mum.

Mum put Little Ted into bed.

She got some
stuffing.

Then she got some thread.

Mum fixed Little Ted.

But she used too much stuffing!

She got some

"I will call him Big Ted!"
said Fred.

Puzzle Time

a

b

Can you find these pictures in the story?

c

d

Which pages are the pictures from?

Turn over for answers!

Answers

The pictures come from these pages:

a. pages 16 and 17

b. pages 20 and 21

c. pages 4 and 5

d. pages 14 and 15

First published in 2010 by
Franklin Watts
338 Euston Road
London
NW1 3BH

Franklin Watts Australia
Level 17/207 Kent Street
Sydney
NSW 2000

A CIP catalogue record for this book is available from the British Library.

ISBN 978 0 7496 9382 4 (hbk)
ISBN 978 0 7496 9395 4 (pbk)

Series Editor: Jackie Hamley
Series Advisors: Dr Hilary Minns and Catherine Glavina
Series Designer: Peter Scoulding

Printed in China

Franklin Watts is a division of Hachette Children's Books, an Hachette UK company. www.hachette.co.uk